My Piggy Bank

By Tom Lewis and Illustrated by K.L. Darnell

Sleeping Bear Press

To Sandi for her unconditional support,
Eliza for her playful reminders of childhood
innocence, and Clayton for providing the
true inspiration behind the words.

Tom Lewis

∾

To my sister, Laura.

K.L. Darnell

Sleeping Bear Press
310 North Main Street, Suite 300
Chelsea, MI 48118
www.sleepingbearpress.com

Sleeping Bear Press is an imprint of The Gale Group, Inc.,
a division of Thomson Learning, Inc.

Printed and bound in Canada.

10 9 8 7 6 5 4 3 2 1

Library of Congress Cataloging-in-Publication Data
Lewis, Thomas, May 3, 1964-
My piggy bank / by Thomas Lewis ; illustrated by Kathryn Darnell.
p. cm.
Summary: With her savings, a little girl buys another piggy bank
so that her first Piggy will have a pal and she can save even more.
ISBN 1-58536-116-X
[1. Piggy banks-Fiction. 2. Saving and investment-Fiction.
3. Stories in rhyme.] I. Darnell, Kathryn, ill. II. Title.
PZ8.3.L5915 My 2003
[E]—dc21   2003010466

My big piggy bank
is exactly that,
it's a pig to keep coins in
and it's really fat.

It was given to me
when I was much younger,
a baby, I think,
but I can't remember.

It's got a big belly,
and when you go near,
you can see my name
painted next to its ears.

For the first couple of years
Piggy sat on my dresser,
up high, out of reach,
where it couldn't be pestered.

Except by my parents
who would thoughtfully drop
all their coins from the day
through the slot on the top.

They said they would give me
a little head start,
until my third birthday
with their coins they'd part.

And just as they said,
on the day I turned three,
they moved Piggy down
to be closer to me.

Now it sat on my nightstand,
within my own reach,
so that I could practice
a lesson they'd teach...

Called "saving my money
for some rainy day"—
I'm not sure what that meant,
but I saved anyway.

A few quarters here,
a dime or two there,
from making my bed
or sweeping the stair.

And before long I saw
Piggy's belly was full,
so down from my nightstand
my Piggy I pulled.

I ran to my Mommy
to tell her the news.
She said she was proud,
then said, "Put on your shoes."

"Let's count all the coins up
and then we'll take half.
You can buy a new toy,
like a bear or giraffe."

"We'll drive to the toy store,"
she said with a laugh,
"You can use your *own* coins,
but remember, just half."

So I jumped in my car seat,
and then off we took.
Shall I buy a new bear?
A giraffe? Or a book?

I looked and I looked,
I just couldn't decide.
Then up high on the shelf
another piggy I spied.

It was shaped much the same
as my other big Piggy,
but softer in color,
and its lines were more wiggly.

My Mom said "But wait,
you have one pig already.
How about something else,
like this teddy named Freddie?"

I said to my Mom,
"Yes, I know I have *one*,
but my Piggy at home
needs a pal, just for fun."

"Besides," I continued,
"I'll save even more.
With *two* pigs I'll save
so much more than before!"

As we drove home I saw
it had started to rain.
Then it dawned on me there
right at Fourth Street and Main.

Could this be the "rainy day"
I'd heard all about?
"I get it!" I said
to my Mom with a shout.

"Is this what you meant
when you said: 'Go and play—
but save all of your coins
for some rainy day'"?

She smiled and said, "Well dear,
it's sort of that way.
Just keep saving your coins
for the next rainy day."

So I save and I save,
it's a fun thing to do.
And I play a whole lot
because I love that too.

I still wonder about
all that "rainy day" talk
as I color with crayons,
or enjoy a nice walk.

But for now I'm just glad
on this day bright with sun,
that I have *two* pigs,
and they're both so much fun.